## DATE DUE

| | | | |
|---|---|---|---|
| | | | |
| | | | |
| | 5/1 | | |
| | | | |
| | | | |
| | | | |
| | | | |
| | | | |
| | | | |
| | | | |
| | | | |
| | | | |
| | | | |
| | | | |
| | | | |
| | | | |

# Mallory
## on
# Board

For A, B, D, and O
With love, from L
—L.B.F.

To my husband Stephen—
in honor of our 10-year wedding
anniversary!
—B. P.

A Special Thank You from the Author:
I'd like to thank all of my friends at Royal Caribbean Cruise
Lines, especially Adam and Cheryl Goldstein, who were so
helpful to me while I was writing this book. My tour aboard
*The Majesty of the Seas* was informative
and so much fun!
I'd also like to thank Barbara Whitehill of The Wedding
Experience. Your knowledge of the industry and willingness
to share it with me was so helpful.
To all of you, my most sincere thanks.
I hope you enjoy the book!

# Mallory
## ON
## Board

by Laurie Friedman
illustrations by Barbara Pollak

Carolrhoda Books, Inc.   Minneapolis • New York

# CONTENTS

# A WORD FROM MALLORY

My name is Mallory McDonald (like the restaurant but no relation), age 9 and 4 months, and right now, I'm standing in my kitchen looking at my refrigerator.

You're probably wondering why I'm looking *at* it and not *in* it. But here's the thing: There's something *on* my refrigerator, and that something is a wedding invitation.

And it's not just for any wedding. It's for the wedding of Mary Ann's mom and Joey's dad. In case you don't know who Mary Ann and Joey are, I'll tell you. They're my best friends! I used to live next door to Mary Ann, until I moved to Fern Falls and moved next door to Joey.

You're probably wondering how their parents

met each other, so I'll tell you that too. When Mary Ann and her mom came to visit, Colleen (Mary Ann's mom) met Frank (Joey's dad) and they spent some time (not that much, if you ask me) getting to know each other and then, POOF, just like that, they decided to get married.

And that's why there's a wedding invitation on my refrigerator. If you look at it carefully, you'll see two things:

#1 The wedding is on the *Sea Queen*, which is a great big cruise ship that we're all going on together.

#2 Frank and Colleen aren't the only ones getting married. Their families are getting married too. I didn't even know families could get married, but they can. It says it in silver and white, right on the invitation.

Even though I'm super excited about going on a great big cruise ship, I'm not super excited about my two best friends becoming part of the same family.

To sum it up in ship talk, I'd say *I'm sunk!*

Mr. Frank Winston
and Ms. Colleen Martin

Invite you to join them and their children,
Mary Ann, Joey, and Winnie,
As they set sail aboard the Sea Queen.

Please share a special moment
In all of their lives
As they and their families
Unite in marriage.

The Beating Hearts Chapel
Wednesday, on the ship, 3 P.M.

~ ~ ~

Dinner in the Dining Room
Dancing and Celebration to follow
In the Tuxedo Lounge

# SPRING BREAK

If Joey and I entered a talking contest,
I know for sure he'd win.

"I'm so excited!" he says for what must
be the fifty-millionth time.

I want to say, *"I know you're so excited . . .
because you've told me fifty million times,"* but I
don't.  I shift my backpack from one
shoulder to the other and keep walking to
Fern Falls Elementary.

Anything, even taking a math test,
would be better than listening to Joey tell

me how excited he is that we're all going on a cruise together so his dad can marry Colleen.

And Joey's not the only one who's excited.

"This cruise is going to be amazing!" says my older brother, Max. "There are three pools, a skating rink, and a rock-climbing wall on the ship."

"There's a salon too," says Joey's sister, Winnie. "And I get to get my hair done for the wedding."

I look at Winnie. Even though she never looks excited about anything, she actually looks like she's pretty excited to go on a ship and get her hair done in a salon.

Joey high-fives Max and Winnie. "I'm so excited," he says for the fifty-millionth-and-one time.

I look down at the sidewalk as we walk.

It's not that I'm not excited about the cruise. I'm very excited about going on the ship. It's just that I'm worried about what things will be like when Frank and Colleen are actually married, and Winnie and Joey and Mary Ann are all part of the same family. And I thought that was something Joey was worried about too.

I pull on Joey's arm so he slows down. "Aren't you worried about what it will be like when your dad marries Colleen?" I ask as Max and Winnie walk ahead of us.

Joey shakes his head, like he doesn't ever remember being worried about that. "They haven't even gotten married yet, and already everything is so cool. We're

going on a cruise, and Dad is always in a good mood."

I follow Joey as he walks through the gates of Fern Falls Elementary. "There's only one thing I'm worried about," he says.

Even though Joey is one of my best friends, in a weird way I'm kind of glad to know there's something bothering him. "What's that?" I ask in my nicest *you'll-feel-*

*better-if-you-talk-about-it* voice.

Joey grins. "How I'm going to make it through one more day of school before Spring Break officially begins." He laughs as we walk through the door of Room 310.

I try to laugh back, like I feel *exactly* the same way he does, but this is one break I'm just not sure I'm ready for.

"Everyone come in and take your seats, please," says Mrs. Daily. "It's our last day for a week and we have a couple of important things to do before the break."

Everyone groans, like no one is in the mood to do anything important, but Mrs. Daily smiles. "The first thing we're going to do is share with the class what we're all doing over Spring Break. Who wants to go first?" she asks.

Joey's hand shoots into the air.

"I'm going on a cruise," he says when

Mrs. Daily calls on him.

"Cool," says Pete. "I wish I could go on a cruise."

"There's more," says Joey.

Then he tells the class that his dad is getting married on the cruise, and that he's marrying my best friend's mom, and that my family is going on the cruise too.

When he says that, everyone turns around and looks at me.

"Wow!" says Danielle. "You're so lucky you get to go on a cruise too."

"With your best friend," says Arielle. She sighs and looks at Danielle. "I wish we could do that."

"Me too," says April. "The only place

I'm going is to my grandmother's house."

"I'm not going anywhere," says Zack. "My grandmother is coming to my house."

I try to listen while everyone talks about where they're going and what they're doing over Spring Break, but my mind is stuck on one thing. And it isn't a swimming pool or a salon or a rock-climbing wall.

The only thing I can think about is my best friends' parents getting married and my best friends becoming one family.

I put my head down on my desk. While I'm busy wondering if Mary Ann and Joey will still be my best friends after they become stepbrother and stepsister, someone taps me on the shoulder.

When I look up, my desk mate, Pamela, passes me a note.

I unfold it and start reading.

Mallory,
You're so lucky you get to go on a cruise!
All I'm doing is practicing for my violin recital.
You're going to have so much fun!
Bon Voyage! (That means have a good time.)
Pamela

I refold the note and smile at Pamela.

Going on a cruise is definitely more fun than practicing for a violin recital. I just wish I wasn't going because Frank and Colleen are getting married.

I do what I do whenever I wish for something and I want it to come true. I pretend like I'm throwing a wish pebble into the wish pond on my street.

The wish I'd like to make is that Frank and Colleen weren't getting married, but I know there's no way *that* wish will come true, so I make a different wish.

*I wish, no matter what, that Mary Ann and Joey will always be my best friends.*

I think about my wish all morning while we do math and science and spelling. I think about it while we eat lunch. And I think about it while we pack up our backpacks at the end of the day to leave for a week.

"Good-bye boys and girls!" Mrs. Daily says to the class when the bell rings. "Have a nice break and be prepared to write about it when you return."

"Anchors aweigh!" Mrs. Daily says to Joey and me as we're leaving the classroom.

"What does that mean?" Joey asks Mrs. Daily.

She smiles. "It means that soon the

anchor will go up, your ship will sail, and when it does, I hope you both have a wonderful time."

"Thanks," Joey says to Mrs. Daily.

I thank her too. I just hope when the anchor goes up, we'll all be in for five days of smooth sailing.

# READY OR NOT!

"Rise and shine, Sweet Potato!" Mom kisses my forehead and puts something into my hand that feels like an envelope. "Special delivery!" she says.

I rub away my sleepies and look at the envelope. "It's from Mary Ann."

Mom picks up a T-shirt off of my floor and dumps it into my hamper. "Even though we're going on the cruise tomorrow, you still have to keep your room neat."

I roll my eyes. "MOOOOOOOM!" I say her name like it's ten syllables and not just one. "I don't have time to clean my room. I have to get ready. I have to decide what to wear and call Mary Ann so we can pack matching clothes."

Just thinking about my best friend and me wearing matching clothes makes me smile. "Everything Mary Ann and I bring can match," I tell Mom. "Bathing suits, sun glasses, hats, pajamas, dresses. It's going to be so much fun."

Mom pats me on the head. "Why don't you read your letter, then come eat breakfast. We'll all start getting ready after that."

I sit up in bed and pull my cat, Cheeseburger, into my lap. I can't wait to read my letter. Maybe Mary Ann's already started thinking about all of the matching things we can bring on the ship too. I rip open the envelope, take out the letter, and start reading.

Dear Mallory,

By the time you get this letter we will almost be on our cruise, and guess what . . . I AM SO, SO, SO EXCITED TO GO ON THIS CRUISE!!!

I bet you are too. We're going to have tons of fun!

There is so much to do on the *Sea Queen*, and guess what? My mom said I don't even have to have a bedtime while we are on the cruise. I can stay up as late as I want! Isn't that great? You should ask your mom if you can do that too. Maybe we can have an all-night pajama party! Doesn't that sound like fun, fun, fun!?!

OK, here's a good packing tip for you:
Bring lots of bathing suits. We will need them.
3 pools! WOW! WOW! WOW! (That was
one WOW for each pool.)

Also, what are you wearing to the wedding?
I wish we could match like we always do, but
I'm matching Winnie. (We are wearing pink
dresses.)

OK, see you soon, soon, soon!

Ahoy Matey! (I think that means *I can't
wait* in ship talk.)

Mary Ann

"Mallory, hurry up!" I hear Mom calling
me.

I crumple up my letter into a little ball
and throw it from my bed to the trash can
by my desk. It lands on the floor. I know

Mom would tell me to clean it up, but I don't.

Even though an all-night pajama party sounds great, it's hard to think about that when all I can think about is Mary Ann and Winnie wearing matching dresses. Mary Ann and I are supposed to match, not Mary Ann and Winnie.

I shove my feet into my fuzzy duck slippers and walk down the hall into the kitchen for breakfast. Mom and Dad are

Girls Who Match

Yes!

NOT!

drinking coffee. Even though we're not leaving for the cruise until tomorrow, Dad looks like he's ready to go today.

"Who's ready to cruise?" he asks in an *I-bet-you're-as-excited-as-I-am* voice.

I take a banana out of the bowl on the table and sit down.

Max walks into the kitchen. "Nice shirt," he says to Dad. He shoves a doughnut into his mouth. "I can't wait until tomorrow."

Dad smiles at Max, even though the front of his shirt is covered in doughnut crumbs. "That's the spirit," he says to Max. Then he looks at me. "You're awfully quiet this morning. Aren't you excited to go on the cruise?"

"Sure," I say. But I guess my *sure* doesn't sound too convincing.

Mom puts her coffee cup down on the counter, then reaches over and feels my

25

forehead. "Mallory, is something bothering you?"

I roll my banana peel into a little ball and dump it in the trash. Then I walk over to the refrigerator and take Frank and Colleen's wedding invitation off of the door. I point to the part about the special ceremony for their families to become one.

"This is what's bothering me," I tell Mom. "I'm excited about going on the cruise, but it's hard to be excited about your best friends becoming part of the same family."

Mom and Dad look at each other.

"Mallory," says Dad. "Frank and Colleen are getting married, and Joey and Mary Ann and Winnie are going to become a family."

I look down at my fuzzy duck slippers. "Joey and Mary Ann and Winnie aren't supposed to be in the same family. They're

supposed to be in different families."

"Sweet Potato," says Mom.

But before she can say anything else about them all becoming a family, I tell Mom what Mary Ann wrote in her letter about her and Winnie wearing matching dresses to the wedding. "Mary Ann and I are supposed to match. Not Mary Ann and Winnie."

Mom puts her arm around me. "It's just a dress. When Mary Ann moves to Fern Falls and lives next door to you, you can wear matching clothes whenever you want to."

I pick a fuzz ball off of my pajamas. "I hope when Mary Ann moves to Fern Falls she'll still want to be my best friend. What if she and Winnie and Joey become best friends?"

Dad pulls me close to him. "I know this is

hard for you, but I want you to think about it from Mary Ann and Winnie and Joey's point-of-view. This is a very special time in their lives. Their parents are getting married. They're your friends. They'll always be your friends. You need to show them that you're happy for them."

I nod my head like I'm going to try. But it's not going to be easy.

Dad rumples my hair like he approves of my head nod, then he reaches into a bag that he has on the counter. "I have something for you and Max." Dad hands each of us a small box wrapped in blue tissue paper.

Max rips the paper off of his box. "A camera!" says Max.

I unwrap my box slowly. "I got one too."

"You each get your own so you can take lots of pictures on the ship," says Dad.

"Mom and I want this cruise to be something you'll always remember."

Max turns his camera over in his hand, and reads the directions on the back of the box. "Thanks!" he says. "I know I'm going to always remember this cruise."

"Thanks," I say. I know I'm going to always remember this cruise too. I just hope my memories will be good ones.

Mom takes the plate of doughnuts off of the table. "We have things to do," she says. Then she picks up a list off the counter and starts giving everybody jobs.

"Harry, you get the

suitcases out of the garage. I'm going next door to see how the Winstons are coming along. Max and Mallory, I put some of your clothes for the trip on your desks. You can start folding and putting things in your suitcases."

"Aye, aye, Captain!" Dad salutes Mom like she's the captain of the ship giving everyone their orders.

I go to my room and start folding clothes like Mom told me to. I fold bathing suits. Shorts. Shirts.

I look at the dress Mom and I bought for me to wear to the wedding. It's yellow, with a bow on the side. I loved it when we bought it. But thinking about Mary Ann and Winnie in their matching pink dresses and me in this one makes me think of an ice cream sundae. Mary Ann and Winnie are scoops of strawberry ice cream in the middle and I'm the banana on the side.

I shove the dress and the beige shoes that Mom made me get to wear with it into my suitcase. Then I plop down on the bed next to Cheeseburger. "I wish you could come with me," I whisper in her ear.

But Cheeseburger doesn't whisper anything back. She's busy sleeping.

I pretend like I'm a cat. I close my eyes and try to go to sleep. But I can't because I can hear Max in the next room.

I walk into his room and plop down on his bed. Even though it never does any good to talk to Max, I try.

"How would you feel if your two best friends' parents were getting married and they were becoming part of the same family?" I ask.

Max tosses a pair of shorts into his suitcase like he's throwing a basketball

through a hoop. "You're lucky," he says.
"Maybe one day they'll move away to
Antarctica and you'll never have to see
either one of them again." Max laughs, like
he just told the funniest joke in the world.

But I don't think it's funny at all. He
might not like my best friends, but I do.

Max picks up a pile of shoes off of the
floor and dumps them into his suitcase.
"Ready or not, we're leaving tomorrow," he
says.

I watch while Max snaps his suitcase shut
and pats the top of it.

At least one of us is ready.

# WELCOME ABOARD!

"Welcome aboard!" A lady in a white sailor's uniform and a nametag that says *Candace, Official Photographer of the Sea Queen* pulls me by the arm until I'm standing under a plastic palm tree. She sticks a red-and-white striped inner tube into my hands.

"Smile big for your official *Welcome-aboard-the-Sea-Queen*-photo, and say cheese . . . *burger,*" she adds with a laugh.

Mom, Dad, Max, Joey, Frank, Grandpa Winston, Colleen, Mary Ann, and Mary Ann's aunts, Alice and Emily, who happen to be identical twins, all smile big and say *cheeseburger*, while Candace takes our picture. Even Winnie, who never smiles, lets the corners of her mouth turn up just a little.

I smile big too, even though saying *cheeseburger* makes me think of my cat, who is staying with our neighbor Mrs. Black while I'm gone.

It's exciting to be on a great big ship, and I think about what Dad said before we left. This is a special time for Joey and Winnie and Mary Ann, and I'm trying to be happy for them.

"OK," says Frank when Candace is done taking the group shot. "Now let's take one of just the family."

He pulls Colleen beside him and lines up Mary Ann and Joey and Winnie in front of them. They all smile when Candace tells them to.

"This will be our first family photo!" Colleen says.

Just thinking about their first family photo makes me think of other things they will do together for the first time.

*First family picnic. First family horseback ride. First family wedding . . . which will be in exactly three days.*

I try to keep the big smile on my face, but it's not so easy to do when I think about all of the fun things my friends are going to be doing together without me.

"Don't they make a nice-looking family?" Mary Ann's Aunt Alice says to my mom.

Mom nods her head, like she agrees that they do.

Max laughs. "I feel sorry for Joey and Winnie," he says to me. "Who would want to have Birdbrain as a stepsister?"

I give Max a dirty look. He knows that I hate when he calls my best friend *Birdbrain.* "I don't feel sorry for Joey or Winnie at all," I tell him. "I would love to have Mary Ann as a stepsister."

Max snorts like he can't think of anything worse.

Someone taps me on the shoulder. I ignore Max's snorting and turn around.

"First time on a cruise ship?" a man wearing white shorts, a white shirt, and a nametag that says *Felix, Cruise Director* asks me.

I nod my head.

He looks down at a clipboard he's carrying. "And you are?"

"Mallory McDonald," I tell Felix.

Felix makes a check on his clipboard and smiles at me. "You're here with the Winstons and the Martins."

"That's us," says Frank.

Everyone walks over to where I'm standing with Felix. He starts asking everyone's names and makes more checks on his clipboard as he finds out who's who in our group.

"Welcome aboard the *Sea Queen!* I see you're all here for a special celebration."

Alice and Emily put their arms around Colleen. "Our sister is getting married on the ship," they tell Felix.

Colleen reaches for Frank's hand.

Felix grins. "Congratulations. I can't think of a better place to be married. And until the big day arrives, there's plenty to do on board the ship."

He hands everyone big packets with the ship's logo on the outside. "There's information in your packets that tells you all about the ship."

Joey rips open his packet and starts reading. "I can't believe there are three pools on this ship," he says. "I can't wait to check them out. I love to swim!"

"I LOVE to swim too!" says Mary Ann.

I look at Mary Ann. I give her an *I-know-you-like-to-swim-but-since-when-do-you-love-to-swim?* look.

Mary Ann ignores my look. "We should swim every day," she says to Joey.

I watch while Joey high-fives Mary Ann, like that's the best idea he's ever heard.

"Why don't we go now?" says Mary Ann.

Felix laughs. "I think you should all go check out your state rooms first, then maybe you can go for a swim before dinner."

"Can we do that?" Joey asks his dad.

"Please!" says Mary Ann.

"I don't see why not," says Frank.

"YEAH!" Joey and Mary Ann shout at the same time, like going swimming is going to be so much fun.

It's not that I don't think swimming sounds like fun, but I do think it would have

been nice if they had asked me if that was what I wanted to do.

Felix clears his throat, like he has an important announcement to make. "As the son of the groom, there's a special surprise waiting for you in your state room," he says to Joey. He looks down at his list. "There's also something for Winnie and Mary Ann."

I wait for him to add my name to that list, but he doesn't. I'd like to tell him that even though my parents aren't getting married, I like special surprises too. But I don't.

I know if I did, Dad would tell me that I'm supposed to be happy for Joey and Mary Ann and Winnie because this is a special time for them. I'm trying to be happy for them, but it's not so easy when their name is on the special surprise list and mine isn't.

"Why don't we all go to our rooms," says

Dad. "We can unpack and freshen up, and then meet at the pool on the top deck."

"Great idea," says Colleen.

We all walk in the direction Felix points us to.

Colleen stops in front of room 515. "Here's our room," she says to Mary Ann, Alice, and Emily. She slips her key into the lock. "Who wants to come in and look?"

We all follow her into the room. It's little, but it's cozy. There's a room with beds for Colleen, Alice, and Emily, and there's another little room connected to it with a cot for Mary Ann and a little table.

"Look!" says Mary Ann, pointing to a big basket of cookies on the table. She hops over the cot and reads the card on top of the basket. "For Mary Ann, daughter of the bride. Welcome aboard! Compliments of the *Sea Queen* Crew."

"That must be the special surprise Felix was talking about," says Joey.

Mary Ann takes a chocolate chip cookie out of the basket and pops it into her mouth. "Mmmm!" she says. "This ship has good surprises."

"I hope we got the same thing," says Joey.

We all follow him down the hall to the Winstons' room. It looks a lot like Mary Ann's room, except there are two cookie baskets on the table.

Winnie reads the cards. "For Winnie, daughter of the groom. For Joey, son of the groom."

"Wow! What a way to welcome us on board." Joey throws a cookie up in the air.

When he catches it in his mouth, Frank laughs. "I'm sure we're all in for five days of fun."

I think about the Winston family photo
that Mary Ann, Joey, and Winnie all took
together.  I think about the cookie baskets
they had waiting for them in their rooms.  I
think about the plan that Joey and Mary
Ann made to go swimming.  When I think
about these things, the thing I think is that
none of these things included me.

I sure hope Frank was right when he said
we're *all* in for five days of fun.

# CRUISE BLUES

"Aren't you coming back in?" asks Joey.

I shake my head *no*. I've been in the pool so long my fingers look like raisins. I wrap a towel around myself and plop down in a deck chair. If I stay in the pool any longer, I'm scared my whole body will look like a giant raisin.

I roll over in the lounge chair I'm sitting in and put a copy of today's *Cruise News*, the official daily newspaper of the *Sea Queen*, over my face to keep the sun out of my eyes.

*Cruise News* tells about all the great stuff that happens on the ship each day. But if I was the person in charge of writing the newspaper, I'd have to call it *Cruise Blues* because the only stuff that's happened to me today hasn't been so great.

I try not to think about the *not-so-great* stuff, and instead, squeeze my eyes shut and make a wish. *I wish this cruise will start improving . . . immediately!*

But the only immediate thing that happens is that someone jerks *Cruise News* off of my face. "Hey, Paper Face," says Max. "Get up. Dad says it's time to get ready for dinner."

I follow Max back to our state room.

"Dad says we're going to the Italian Buffet in the dining room, and then to the *Welcome Aboard The Sea Queen* show. Pretty cool, huh?" says Max.

I nod my head *yes*, that I do think it's cool. Then I think about the wish I just made. Maybe it will start coming true tonight.

After we all get dressed, we knock on the Winstons' door and the Martins' door to see if they're ready to go to dinner. We all walk to the dining room together.

When we get there, Felix is waiting by the door to greet us.

"Let's see," he says. "The Winston and Martin families are at the Windjammer table, and the McDonald family is at the High Tides table."

I wrinkle my nose. I don't like the sound of the Winston and Martin families at one table and the McDonald family at another.

"The Windjammer table is right over here," says Felix, pointing to a table on his left. He looks at Joey and Mary Ann. "That's where your families will be seated for dinner every night on the ship."

Then he points to a table all the way across the room. "And the High Tides table is over there." Felix looks down at his clipboard. "Mallory, your family will be sitting with the Burgers, a very nice family from Idaho who has a daughter your age and a son Max's age."

I look in the center of the room at all of

the Italian food. Even though I haven't started eating, I feel like I just swallowed a whole pizza. "How come we can't sit with the Martins and the Winstons?" I ask.

"Because all of the tables hold eight people. Since they already have eight at their table, we put your family with another family of four," Felix explains.

"We'll all sit together at the show tonight," Joey says to me.

"OK," I say like *OK, that makes sense to me.* I'm trying to make it make sense to me, but if we came on the trip to be with the Martins and the Winstons, I don't see how it makes sense that we don't get to sit together at dinner.

I watch while Joey and Mary Ann sit down at their table, and then I follow Mom and Dad to ours.

"Hi!" says a girl when I get to our table.

She pulls out the chair next to her, and I sit down. "I'm Tammy Burger," she says. Then she points to a boy at the table. "This is my brother, Timmy. You must be Mallory, and you must be Max," she says pointing to me and my brother. "Felix told us all about you. I know your last name is McDonald, which is really cool, because ours is Burger, and that means we have a lot in common. McDonald. Burger. McDonald's serves burgers. Get it? And . . ."

But before Tammy can say anything else, her brother, Timmy, interrupts her. "In case you haven't noticed, Tammy likes to talk," he says. "She also likes to watch TV."

"I don't like to watch TV. I LOVE to watch TV!" says Tammy. "Right before we came on the cruise, I saw this totally sad show about these two girls who are best friends. They go on a cruise together. And get this: one of the girls makes a new best friend and completely forgets about her old best friend. Isn't that sad?"

"Totally," I tell Tammy. I came on this cruise with my best friends. But what if my best friends become best friends? That

would be totally sad.

"Who wants to make a plate?" asks Dad. He leads the way over to the buffet. While everyone is busy picking pizza or pasta, I think about the show Tammy saw.

I take some spaghetti and a breadstick and follow everyone back to the table. "So what happened to the girl in the show who

lost her best friend?" I ask Tammy.

Tammy sticks her fork into a meatball. "She makes a new friend," says Tammy.

I try to smile back, but I feel like I'm going to choke on my breadstick. I don't want new friends. I want to keep my old ones.

I look across the dining room at Mary Ann. She and Joey are busy twirling spaghetti around their forks and laughing.

I think about the wish I made earlier. It doesn't seem like it's coming true yet.

When we're done with dinner, we all go to the *Sea Queen Theater* for the *Welcome Aboard* show.

"Mallory, over here!" Joey waves to me from across the theater. "Mary Ann and I saved a seat for you," he says when I get to them.

I sit down between them.

Maybe my wish is coming true after all.

The lights go down. The captain of the ship, Captain Nate, walks onto the stage and welcomes everyone aboard the *Sea Queen*. He tells us all about fun stuff to do on the boat, like water activities, the ice cream sundae bar, and T-shirt making. "You'll even get to spend the day on our private tropical island," he says.

"I can't wait to make T-shirts," Mary Ann whispers in my ear.

"I can't wait to go on an island," Joey whispers in my other ear.

I nod. Both things sound like tons of fun. I cross my toes. Maybe this cruise is improving.

We watch as some singers and dancers welcome all of the parents and the kids on the boat. Then one of the singers makes an announcement. "We have some very special guests on the ship whose parents are getting married," says the dancer. "Will Mary Ann Martin and Joey and Winnie Winston please come up onto the stage?"

I stick my finger in my ear to make sure I'm not hearing things.

Mary Ann and Joey and Winnie walk up onto the stage. They sit in glow-in the-dark chairs while the singers and dancers sing a *congratulations* song.

I sit quietly in my regular chair and look

at the empty seats next to me.  One
minute my best friends were on both sides
of me.  The next minute they're gone.

When I imagined what this cruise would
be like, that's not what I had in mind.

When the show is over, Mary Ann and
Joey come back over to me.  Even though
the night didn't start out so great, maybe
it can end great.

"Hey," I say to Mary Ann.  "Do you want
to have the all-night pajama party?"

Mary Ann yawns.  "Maybe another
night," she says.  "I'm tired from
swimming."

Mary Ann never says *no* to a pajama
party.  I think about the wish I made.  So
far, it doesn't seem like it's coming true.  I
make a new wish.

*I wish this cruise will start improving . . .*
*tomorrow.*

# ICE CREAM & T-SHIRTS

"I scream! You scream! We all scream for ice cream!" Joey and Mary Ann chant together.

Frank smiles, even though Joey and Mary Ann are screaming at the top of their lungs. "T-shirts first, then ice cream," he says.

It sounds like a fun plan to me. I can already tell that today is going to be better than yesterday.

I follow Frank, Joey, Winnie, Mary Ann, Mom, Dad, and Max into the T-shirt making room. Colleen is already there making a T-shirt.

"Look," she says when we walk in. She holds up a white T-shirt with blue writing and little blue sailboats on it. The words *Winston Crew* are written across the front. "Isn't it cute?" says Colleen. "It's the official Winston family T-shirt."

"We can all make them," says Frank.

I look around the room. I'm not sure who Frank means when he says *all*. Joey, Winnie, Mary Ann, Frank, and Colleen can *all* make *Winston Crew* T-shirts. They're all part of the Winston crew. But I'm not. I watch as they crowd around Colleen and she shows them how she made the little sailboats.

Dad holds up a T-shirt. "Mallory, Max, over here. You guys can help us decide how to decorate our T-shirts."

"Maybe we should put *McDonald Mania* on it," says Mom.

"Maybe we can put little inner tubes all over it too," Max says. He rolls his eyes like anything having to do with inner tubes is dumb.

I don't know if inner tubes are dumb or not, but what I do know is that I feel like I just swallowed one.

I thought making T-shirts would be fun, but I don't want to make a *McDonald Mania* T-shirt while Joey and Winnie and Mary Ann all make *Winston Crew* ones.

Even though making T-shirts won't be as much fun as I thought it would be, I take one from Dad and put the little inner tube stencil on top of it and spray paint over it.

"Stand next to Mom and Max," says Dad. He takes a picture of us making *McDonald Mania* T-shirts.

"Mal, you should get your camera out later," says Dad. "Take some pictures."

"I will," I tell Dad. Hopefully, later, there will be some things I want to photograph, and hopefully, these things won't have anything to do with Frank and Colleen getting married and the Winstons and the Martins becoming one big happy family. So far, it seems like everything has been about that.

When we're done with our T-shirts, everyone slips theirs on, and Dad takes more pictures.

"Who's ready for a swim and then ice cream sundaes?" asks Frank.

Everyone says that sounds great, and I think it does too. But I can't help

wondering: Is there going to be an official Winston family swimming stroke and an official Winston family ice cream sundae?

As we walk back to the pool, I try not to think about that, and instead, I think about the rest of the cruise.

Tomorrow, we're getting off of the boat and going to a tropical island.

The day after that, Frank and Colleen are getting married.

The day after that, we go home.

We only have three days left on the cruise ship, and I really want them to be good. I close my eyes and pretend I'm at the wish pond. Even though I've made a lot of wishes lately, I make another one.

*I hope the last three days of the cruise will be more fun than the first two.*

I sure hope my wish comes true.

# ISLAND NIGHTMARE

"C'mon, Mallory," says Max. "You have to choose."

"And make it quick," says Winnie. "We only have four hours on this island, and we've already wasted fifteen minutes waiting for you to decide."

The problem is . . . making this decision isn't easy. Max, Timmy, and Tammy are going to *Waves of Fun,* a water park, which sounds like tons of fun.

But Mary Ann, Joey, and Winnie are going shopping to pick out wedding presents for Frank and Colleen. Even though I'd rather go to a water park, I don't want to *not* spend the only day we have on a real island without my best friends.

"I'm going to do eenie, meenie, miney, mo," I say out loud.

Mary Ann grabs my hand. "You don't need to do eenie, meenie, miney, mo," she says. "You'll help us shop, and when we're done, we'll go to the water park."

I let Mary Ann lead me down the palm-tree lined path towards the island stores.

"Bye!" Tammy waves to me as she and Timmy and Max go in the opposite direction. "Have fun!" she calls out over her shoulder.

I wave back. As we walk into a store

called *The Island Outlet,* I can't help thinking
that I hope I do have fun. I look around at
all of the tables of T-shirts and baseball
caps and coffee mugs. Then I make a wish.
*I sure hope Winnie and Mary Ann and Joey
pick quick, because I can't wait to get to
Waves of Fun.*

"OK," Winnie says like she's the oldest so
she's in charge. "Let's find something for
your mom first," she says to Mary Ann.
"Then we'll get something for our dad."

"Great!" says Mary Ann.  She smiles at
Winnie like it's fine that she's in charge.

"We decided we would shop for the
presents together since I know what my
mom likes and they know what their dad
likes," she says to me.

"I get it," I say like I *do* get it.  But here's
what I don't get:  I thought Mary Ann didn't
even like Winnie, and all of a sudden, she's
acting like she's glad she's going to have a
new older sister who thinks she's in charge.

I was worried that Mary Ann and Joey
were becoming good friends, but now I
have a new worry:  What if Mary Ann and
Winnie become good friends too?

As Winnie starts holding up T-shirts and
candles for Mary Ann to see, I feel like
there's a beehive in my stomach, and the
bees in the hive won't stop buzzing.

"What do you think of this?"  Winnie

picks up a T-shirt with a picture of an island on it.

Mary Ann shakes her head. "My mom never wears T-shirts."

Joey holds up a coffee mug. "Would your mom like this?"

Mary Ann shakes her head *no* and tells Joey that her mom already has a whole cabinet full of coffee mugs.

I watch while Joey and Mary Ann and Winnie look through displays of hats and shorts and T-shirts and glasses and mugs.

I feel like a thousand more bees just joined the hive. I think about what Dad said, about being a patient, good friend. But watching my best friends pick out wedding gifts for each other's parents is really hard.

"How about this?" asks Winnie. She holds up a paperweight.

"No." Mary Ann shakes her head. "I don't see anything here I think my mom would like. Why don't we try to find something for your dad."

Mary Ann holds up a magnet, some socks, and a bag of chocolates, but Joey and Winnie shake their head each time, like none of those items are quite right for their dad.

"Maybe we should go to another store," says Winnie.

I don't want to go to another store, I want to go to a water park. Maybe what I should do is help my friends so we can get to that park as soon as possible.

I hold up His and Her flip-flops. "How about these?" I say in my *I-can't-imagine-a-better-wedding-present* voice.

But Mary Ann, Winnie, and Joey all shake their heads *no,* like they couldn't imagine a worse present.

"Mallory, this is really important," Mary Ann says in a *finding-the-perfect-presents-may-not-be-important-to-you-but-it's-important-to-us* voice. "Do you want to come with us to another store or not?"

"Sure." I nod my head *yes,* like that's exactly what I want to do. But as we walk out of *The Island Outlet* and into *The Island Market,* all I can think is that it's not at all what I want to be doing.

It's not just that I want to go to the water park. I do, but I can't help feeling like my friends don't even care that I came along with them. Part of me feels like they'd be happier if I hadn't come.

"What do you think of this store?" Mary Ann asks Winnie.

"It looks pretty good," says Winnie.

But I think it looks the same as the last

store. They have all of the same hats, shorts, T-shirts, glasses, and mugs.

I sit down in a chair at the front of the store and read through a brochure that Felix gave us about stuff to do on the island. I hope that by the time I'm finished reading it, Mary Ann, Winnie, and Joey will be through finding the perfect gifts for Frank and Colleen.

But when I finish, they're still shopping. I read the brochure again . . . and again . . . and again. I read it four times.

Mary Ann walks over to me. "Mallory, we didn't find anything. We're going to go next door to *The Island Outfitter.*"

"Oh," I say to Mary Ann.

I guess my *oh* doesn't sound very enthusiastic, because Mary Ann gives me a funny look. "Don't you want us to find something?"

Actually, I do. I want them to find something even more than they want to find something. I think they're enjoying this shopping trip. I'm the one who wants to get to the water park. I pop out of my chair and follow Mary Ann. "Of course I do!" I say.

I look at my watch as we walk into *The Island Outfitter.* We've spent the whole morning shopping and haven't found anything yet. I think about Max and Timmy and Tammy at *Waves of Fun.* I bet they're having waves of fun.

When we get inside, Mary Ann and Winnie and Joey start looking at all of the merchandise, and I start looking at my watch.

I look up when I hear a scream.

"Look at these!" Mary Ann is bouncing around like she finally found the perfect gift. She holds up matching straw hats with shells all over them. "Aren't they cute?"

"I love them!" says Joey.

"Me too," says Winnie. "I think our parents will love them."

I watch while they pay the cashier. I wait while the cashier gift wraps them. I wait some more while Mary Ann and Joey and Winnie all sign the cards. Somehow I know without looking at my watch that we don't have enough time to go to *Waves of Fun* before we have to be back on the ship.

When Mary Ann and Joey and Winnie are done signing cards, we all walk outside. Max and Timmy and Tammy are walking towards us. "You better hurry if you want to make it back to the ship," says Max.

We follow them down the path. "How was shopping?" Tammy asks me.

But before I can even answer, she starts telling me about this TV show she saw called *Island Nightmare*.

"It was so scary," says Tammy. "It was about these kids who get trapped on a deserted island. When I heard we were going to spend a day on an island, I was kind of scared because I kept thinking about the show."

"Yeah," I say to Tammy, like the show sounds scary.

Tammy pulls her sunglasses down over her eyes and keeps talking. "But we had such a good time today. *Waves of Fun* was amazing. They have four pools and six water slides. Being on this island wasn't anything like *Island Nightmare*."

I nod my head like I'm glad Tammy's day on the island wasn't a nightmare.

I wish I could say the same thing about my own.

# WEDDING DAY

It's only nine o'clock in the morning and I've already learned something. I've learned that on the day of a wedding, people like to ask a lot of questions.

If you're wondering how I learned this, I'll tell you. Today is the day that Frank and Colleen are getting married, and ever since we sat down for breakfast, all Mom and Mary Ann's aunts, Alice and Emily, have done is ask Colleen questions.

*When is she going to start getting ready?*

*Is everything OK with her dress and her shoes? How do the flowers look? Has she spoken to the photographer? Does she need any help? When should we arrive at the chapel?*

When they finally quit asking questions, I push my plate of uneaten pancakes away and ask one of my own. "Who wants to go swimming?"

I wait for Mary Ann or Joey to raise their hands. I know they love to swim. But neither one of them do.

"Mary Ann and I can't go swimming because we're having our hair done for the wedding," says Winnie. She tosses her hair behind her shoulders like she's a movie star who is about to get ready for an important shoot.

"They're going to have matching hairstyles," says Colleen.

I give Mary Ann a *we're-supposed-to-be-the-*

*ones-who-have-matching-hairstyles* look, but Mary Ann looks like she's happy that she's going to match Winnie. Mary Ann is supposed to be my lifelong best friend, but right now, I don't think she's acting like it.

I look at Joey. "I know you're not getting your hair done," I say to him like there's no way he won't be free to swim.

But Joey shakes his head like he's not free at all. "I've got wedding stuff to do," he says.

"Like what?" I ask.

Joey shrugs his shoulders, like whatever he has to do, he's not telling me about it.

Joey is my other best friend, and right now, I don't think he's acting like it either.

I cross my arms across my chest. I'm not too happy that neither one of my best friends wants to do what I want to do.

Mom is the only one who looks like she cares how I'm feeling, and the reason she looks like she cares is because she doesn't like what I'm feeling.

She raises her eyebrows when she talks to me. "Mallory, no one has time to swim today. We all have to get ready for the wedding this afternoon." She gives me one of her *I-hope-you-get-what-I'm-saying* looks.

I do . . . but I don't like it. And I don't think Mom would like it either if her best friends were too busy to do anything she wanted to do.

"It doesn't take *all* day to get ready, does it?" I ask.

Mom looks at me like she can't believe she has to answer that question, but before she can say anything, Colleen does.

"Actually, there's a lot we need to do." Colleen looks like just talking about the preparations makes her happy. "We need to do hair and makeup and get dressed and make sure everything is in order for the ceremony and the party."

Colleen smiles at me, like the *we* she's talking about includes me. But I don't feel like it does. I feel like the *we* means Joey and Mary Ann and the rest of their soon-to-be-family.

Günter Grass    Die Box

Mom stands up from the table. "OK, everyone, we've got a lot to do to be ready for today. Let's get a move on."

I stand up. But I feel like my body doesn't want to move on its own. It's like it's saying *even though this is an important day for my best friends, I don't really want to help them get ready for it.* I feel like Mary Ann and Joey are so busy thinking about what's going on in their own lives, they've forgotten about me.

When everyone gets up from the table, I ask Mom if I can go sit by the pool for a while before I have to get ready.

"I don't see why not," says Mom.

"If you decide to stay there forever, it was nice knowing you," says Max.

I ignore my brother and walk to the deck and find a chair. I sit down by myself, which is fine, because I'm the only person I want to be with right now.

But I'm not by myself for long. Felix pulls up a chair and sits down beside me.

"Mallory, what are you doing all by yourself on such a beautiful day?" he asks with a smile.

"That's a good question," I tell Felix. "But I don't have a good answer." And trying to think of one doesn't make me feel any better.

Felix stops smiling. He gets a serious look on his face. "You know Mallory, I've seen lots of weddings on this ship. It's always nice when two people who love each other get married, but sometimes it's hard for other people."

"I know what you mean," I tell Felix. Then I tell him that I feel like one of those other people.

"Every time I want to do something with

my best friends, they're doing something with each other that doesn't include me. They swim together. They eat dinner together. They make T-shirts together. They shop together. And none of it includes me."

Felix smiles at me like what he's about to say will hopefully cheer me up. "Mallory, we have an old expression we use on the *Sea Queen*. We like to say, 'There are good ships and bad ships, but the best ships are friendships.' "

I tell him about something Mrs. Daily taught us. It's called a third wheel. "A third wheel is like an extra wheel that you don't need," I tell Felix. "And ever since I came on this cruise, I feel like a third wheel when I'm around Mary Ann and Joey."

"Mallory," says Felix, "you can't possibly be a third wheel on a ship because ships don't have wheels." Felix laughs at his joke and then pats me on the head.

I know he's trying to make me feel better. And in a way, I do. Ships don't have wheels, so I guess I can't be a third wheel while I'm on *The Sea Queen*.

But the problem is, I won't be on this ship forever. Soon, Colleen and Frank will be married, and Joey and Mary Ann will be one family.

And then what?

Too bad for me the *questions* side of my brain is full, and the *answers* side is empty.

# TYING THE KNOT

"Do you think Colleen would like it if I sing, 'Here Comes the Bride, Big, Fat, and Wide' as she walks down the aisle?" Max asks Dad.

Dad straightens Max's tie and turns him around so he can see himself in the mirror in our state room. "I think I'll let you answer that question," Dad says. Then he pats Max on the back. "You look very nice in a suit."

"Thanks," says Max. "I've never been to a wedding before. I think it'll be kind of fun to go to one on a cruise ship."

Dad smiles, like he agrees, and straightens his own tie. Then he turns around and looks at me. "Mallory, you look beautiful . . . from the ankles up. Why don't you have your shoes on?"

I stretch my toes. "I don't want to put my shoes on yet. They hurt my feet."

Mom stops putting on lipstick and looks at my bare feet. "Mallory, we're leaving for the ceremony in just a few minutes. You need to finish getting dressed."

I lie down on my bed, like what I want to do is take a nap, not put on my shoes and leave for the ceremony.

"Mallory, you'll wrinkle your dress," says Mom.

But I don't care if my dress gets

wrinkled. In less than an hour, my two best friends will be stepbrother and stepsister.

Dad walks over to my bed and sits down beside me. "Sweet Potato, I know that a lot of things in your world are changing, and I know it's hard for you."

He rubs my back. "Today is a very important day for Mary Ann and Joey. As their best friend, I want you to show them that you're happy for them."

I sit up in bed. "I've tried to be happy for them," I tell Dad. "But it's hard when they keep doing things that don't include me."

Dad pulls me into his lap. "Sometimes things aren't easy." He picks up one of my shoes and pretends like he's trying to shove my foot in it, but my foot is too big for the shoe. "Like getting this shoe on this big foot," he says.

"I don't know which is bigger . . . her foot or her mouth," says Max.

Dad pretends like he's going to throw the shoe at Max, but instead he picks up my other foot and tickles it. "Whatever you do," says Dad, "don't laugh."

But I can't help it. I always laugh when Dad tickles my feet.

He stands up and tosses me my other shoe. "Finish getting dressed, and let's go."

Dad picks up the key off of the dresser.

It's next to the cameras that Mom and Dad gave Max and me before the trip.

"Don't forget these," he says as he hands us each our cameras. "You might want to take some pictures at the party."

I take my camera. I've barely taken any pictures since we got on board the ship. Somehow, I don't think tonight is going to be the night that I start.

Max and I follow Mom and Dad as they walk down the hallway to the chapel. As we cross the deck, my shoes make a loud tapping noise.

When we get to the door of the *Beating Hearts Chapel,* Mom turns around. "Mallory, can you please try to walk a little more quietly, especially when we get inside the chapel?" she asks.

"I'll try," I tell Mom. But I think she's forgotten that she's the one who chose these shoes, and they're not exactly the quiet kind.

When we walk inside the chapel, there are white flowers and candles everywhere.

Felix is waiting by the door. "Everyone looks splendid," he says. He gives each of us a wedding program and shows us to our seats.

He puts Mom and Dad in the second row beside Aunt Alice, Aunt Emily, and Grandpa Winston. He gives Max and me chairs in the row behind them.

I point to the empty first row. "Who's sitting there?" I ask Felix.

But he puts his fingers to his lips as soft organ music starts playing in the background. "You're about to see," he whispers.

Felix walks to the back of the chapel and opens the door. When he does, Captain

Nate enters wearing a white captain's suit and walks up to the front of the room.

He faces the audience and waits.

The music gets a little louder, and Felix opens the door again. This time Joey and Winnie and Mary Ann all walk in together. Winnie and Mary Ann are wearing matching pink dresses and they have

matching hairstyles. They all sit down in the front row.

"Don't the girls look nice in their matching dresses?" Aunt Alice whispers.

Mom nods her head like she agrees that they do.

But I don't agree. Mary Ann and I are the ones who always wear matching dresses. Not Mary Ann and her new stepsister.

I rub my shoes back and forth across the floor. They make a loud, squeaky noise.

Mom puts her fingers to her lips like she wants me to be quiet.

But I don't think it would matter if I sang "Row, Row, Row Your Boat" at the top of my lungs. Just when Mom puts her fingers to her lips, the music gets a lot louder, like someone as important as the President is about to enter the room, and Frank walks in.

He walks to the front of the chapel and

stands beside Captain Nate.

Everyone is smiling. Then the music gets softer again. When it does, Felix opens the door, and Colleen walks down the aisle.

She has on a big white dress and a veil, and she's carrying a huge bouquet of flowers. Everyone watches as she walks slowly up the aisle, then stops when she

gets to the end and faces Frank.

Even though most of me wishes she wasn't marrying Frank, part of me thinks that she makes a beautiful bride.

Mom, Aunt Alice, and Aunt Emily must think so too. Even Grandpa Winston must think so. They all start dabbing their eyes with tissues.

Captain Nate clears his throat like he wants everyone to pay attention. When everyone does, he starts talking.

"Dearly beloved, we are gathered here today to witness the union of this very special couple, Mr. Frank Winston and Ms. Colleen Martin."

I feel like the moment I wasn't waiting for is finally here.

I listen while Captain Nate reads a poem about love.

Next, he asks Frank and Colleen to state the vows of love that they wrote for each other. After they do that, he says that it is time to exchange rings.

He has Frank place the ring he bought for Colleen on her finger. Then he asks Frank to repeat after him. "With this ring, I thee wed," says Captain Nate.

Frank repeats what Captain Nate says,

and then he slips the ring onto Colleen's finger.

Then Captain Nate asks Colleen to do the same thing for Frank.

When they are done exchanging rings, Captain Nate smiles. The smile on his face is almost as big as the hat on his head. "I now pronounce you husband and wife," says Captain Nate. "Frank, you may kiss the bride."

I watch while Frank kisses Colleen.

"Best of luck as you set sail for the rest of your lives together," says Captain Nate.

Everyone in the room claps and smiles.

I clap and smile like I'm happy too. In a way I am. At least the wedding ceremony is over, and I don't have to worry about that anymore.

The only thing left for me to worry about is the rest of their lives.

# A FAMILY CIRCLE

"We're not quite done," says Captain Nate. "We still have one more important ceremony to perform."

He smiles at Mary Ann and Joey and Winnie, who are all sitting in the front row. "I'd like to invite Frank and Colleen's kids up here to join us. It's time to perform the ceremony that unites these two families as one."

I was so busy thinking about Frank and Colleen saying *we do* that I forgot about the *we ALL do* part of the wedding.

I watch while Mary Ann and Joey and Winnie all walk up the aisle to where Frank and Colleen are standing in front of Captain Nate. Frank puts one arm around Winnie and the other one around Colleen. Colleen puts her arm around Mary Ann. They make a big circle.

I draw my own big circle on the floor with my feet.

Mom turns around in her chair and puts her finger to her lips to tell me to be quiet. Even Grandpa Winston turns around like he thinks I should be quiet too.

I try to explain that it wasn't me, it was my shoes, but Captain Nate clears his throat like he's trying to get everyone's attention, especially mine.

"Let's proceed," he says. "Frank, Colleen, Joey, Winnie, Mary Ann, I'd like you to take each other's hands."

I watch while they all hold hands.

I don't know why they have to all marry each other anyway. A wedding is supposed to be about two people getting married, not *two people and all their kids.*

"Let's continue," says Captain Nate.

"Frank, Colleen, Joey, Winnie, Mary Ann, from this day forward you will all be a family. You will be a family in good times and in bad. You will be a family in sickness and in health. You will be there for each other to weather life's ups and downs."

Captain Nate pauses. "I know you've all written a poem expressing your thoughts on becoming a family. I would like to call on each of you to share these thoughts."

Frank pulls a sheet of paper from his pocket. He clears his throat and begins.

*"Family means many things to me.*
*It's faith and love and security."*

Frank passes the sheet of paper to Colleen, who dabs her eyes with a tissue, and picks up where Frank left off.

*"It's a place to go where you will find*
*A loving heart or a word that is kind."*

Colleen passes the paper to Joey, who

continues reading.

"It's a group of people who care what you do.

They like knowing and learning things about you."

Joey hands the paper to Winnie, who takes her turn.

"They like knowing that you're all part of a team.

They like helping you learn, create, grow, and dream."

Winnie passes the paper to Mary Ann, who finishes the poem.

"It's a feeling you get when you're all together.

Our family is something we'll treasure forever."

I watch Mary Ann give the paper back to Frank, who refolds it and slips it back into his pocket.

"I don't know who wrote that poem, but whoever did isn't a very good poet," Max whispers in my ear.

For once, I agree with Max. I didn't like that poem at all, especially the part about forever. Some things are supposed to be forever, like Mary Ann being my oldest best friend, and Joey being my newest best friend. I don't like thinking about Mary Ann and Joey being part of the same family . . . FOREVER!

I kick my heels against the wood floor, and they make a loud noise.

Mom, Grandpa Winston, Aunt Alice, and Aunt Emily all turn around and say *"Shhh!"* at the same time. They look like they're the chorus in a play and they're all saying their part together.

"It was my shoes," I say.

"Then your shoes need to stop making

noise," whispers Mom.

She turns back around and Captain Nate starts talking again. "That was a beautiful poem," he says. "And now, I have a little poem of my own."

Captain Nate clears his throat again and smiles.

*"By the powers vested in me at sea,*
*I now pronounce you a family."*

When he says "*I now pronounce you a family,*" everyone claps and cheers, just like they did when Captain Nate pronounced Frank and Colleen husband and wife.

Everyone but one person . . . and that one person is me. In my opinion, this is nothing to clap about.

Just thinking about Frank and Colleen and Joey and Winnie and Mary Ann becoming a family and having fun together, without me, makes me want to

cry, not clap.

"One last thing before we conclude the service," says Captain Nate. He speaks softly. "Let's all take a moment to be silent. Let's think about all of the good things in store for this family."

Everyone around me stops clapping and cheering. No one says a word, and I don't say anything either. The room is so quiet.

What I don't want to do is think about all of the good things in store for this family. What I do want to do is kick my heels back and forth against the floor.

I kick. Back and forth. Back and forth. I don't know why, but kicking my heels makes me feel better . . . until Mom turns around and looks at me. She gives me a *you-better-stop-that-this-instant-if-you-know-what's-good-for-you-young-lady* look.

So I stop kicking and then, before I even

have a chance to think about what I'm doing, I stand up, grab my purse, my program, and my camera.

The room is still quiet, except for one sound: the clicking of my shoes against the wood floor as I leave the *Beating Hearts Chapel.*

# WISHING FOR THE WISH POND

I run from the wedding chapel all the way to the top deck and plop down in a lounge chair.

Then I wait. I can feel my heart pounding.

I know everyone will follow me. Any minute, Mom and Dad and Mary Ann and Joey and everyone else will find me here. When they do, they'll throw their arms around me and say: *Mallory, we're so happy*

*to see you! Why did you leave? Tell us what's wrong and we're going to do whatever it takes to make you feel better.*

And I'll explain that I don't want Colleen and Frank to be married, and Joey and Mary Ann and Winnie to all be one big family. When I explain how it makes me feel, I know they'll get Captain Nate to undo what he did.

I watch the big clock on the deck.

One minute. Two minutes. Five minutes. No sign of anybody. I can feel my heart slowing down.

Seven minutes. Eight minutes. Ten minutes. I can't believe it's taking this long to find me. Everyone must be looking in all of the wrong places.

Twelve minutes. Fifteen minutes. Where is everybody? Why aren't they looking for me? What if they don't even know I'm gone?

I think about Cheeseburger. She'd know where to find me.

I can feel hot tears starting to form behind my eyes. I blink so they won't fall out. I don't want to be crying when everybody shows up.

Eighteen minutes. I look down at the wedding program I'm still holding.

I can't believe no one has come to find me. I can't believe they care more about a wedding than they care about me. I can feel a tear starting to squeeze out of my eye.

I look down at my camera and my purse and the wedding program in my lap.

I open my purse to get out a tissue, but all I have is a pen and some lip gloss.

I press my hand against my eye to keep the tears inside. I take out my pen and start writing on the back of my wedding program.

I'm so
busy writing,
I don't even
notice when
someone sits
down in the
seat beside me.

"Is this chair
taken?" a male
voice asks.

I look up. "Dad!" I'm
so happy to see him, but he
doesn't look nearly as happy to see me. In
fact, he doesn't look happy at all.

He crosses his arms across his chest.
"Mallory Louise McDonald, you have some
explaining to do. You ran out during the
wedding ceremony and I need to know why."

I hand him the wedding program I've

been writing on. "Read this," I say, "and you'll know why."

Dad looks down at the paper and starts reading.

10 Reasons Why I, Mallory McDonald, Left Frank and Colleen's wedding

#1: I was hot.
#2: The room was stinky.
#3: My chair was hard.
#4: Captain Nate talked too loud.
#5: My shoes hurt.
#6: My dress was itchy.
#7: I thought it was over.
#8: I had to sneeze.
#9: I didn't have anything to do.
#10: Nobody cared if I stayed.

"Mallory, the first nine reasons don't seem like very good reasons," Dad says.

I look down at my list. "They seem like good reasons to me."

"What about the tenth reason?" asks Dad.

"What about it?" I ask.

"I don't think it's true," he says.

Dad might not think it's true, but I do. I start to explain, but when I open my mouth, I feel like I'm going to start crying again. I look down at my purse.

"Mallory, everybody at that wedding cared very much that you were there. Frank and Colleen only invited the people who mean the most to them, and you're one of those people.

"This was a very important moment in the lives of your two best friends, and you weren't there for them," Dad says softly.

I bite down on my tongue. Even though I didn't want to stay at the wedding, part of me feels badly that I left. I try to keep in the tears I've been holding back all day, but they start to run down my cheeks.

One lands on my yellow dress and leaves a mark.

Dad wipes it away with his finger, then he picks me up out of my chair and puts me on his lap. "Sweet Potato," he says.

But before he can say anything else, words start spilling out of my mouth faster than tears are flowing from my eyes.

"I tried to be there for my friends. I tried to be happy and excited for them. And not just today. This whole trip I've tried. But they've been so busy doing what they wanted to do that I don't think they cared if I was happy or excited. I don't even think they cared that I was on this trip."

Dad looks down at me. "Mallory, you know that's not true. Joey and Mary Ann care so much about you. You're their best friend."

I shake my head from side to side, like what Dad is saying isn't the case. "If I was their best friend, I don't think they would have spent all their time on the cruise doing things that didn't include me."

I start telling Dad how I felt when they were making *Winston Crew* T-shirts and shopping for wedding gifts for Frank and Colleen, but Dad stops me.

He tilts my chin up so he's looking at me, and I'm looking at him. "Mallory, sometimes people, even best friends, do things that disappoint us. It doesn't mean they don't care. Sometimes, to have a friend, you have to be a friend, even when you might not like how your friends are acting."

I put my head against Dad's jacket. "I just wish things could be different," I tell him. "I wish I was at home and I could go to the wish pond and make a wish and it would come true."

Dad smiles. "Sometimes we all wish things could be different." He stands up and puts me down on the deck. Then he takes my hand. "Come with me," says Dad. "I have an idea."

We walk over to the railing of the ship. Dad points out to sea. "Why don't you think of the ocean as a great big wish pond."

"I guess I could try," I say.

Dad rumples my hair. "Go ahead. Make a wish and let's see what happens."

I squeeze my eyes shut like I would if I

was making a wish at the wish pond. *I wish my best friends will always be my best friends, no matter what happens.*

"Feel better?" Dad asks when I open my eyes.

I shrug my shoulders. I'm not sure if I do. A cold wind blows across the deck of the boat, and I shiver.

Dad takes off his jacket and slips it over my shoulders. "C'mon," he says. "We're having dinner with the Captain, then we have a party to go to."

"But Dad, isn't everyone going to want to know why I left the wedding?"

Dad smiles down at me. "I wouldn't worry about that. Everyone is in a party mood."

I take Dad's hand. But before I walk away, I look at the ocean and make one more wish. *I wish I was in a party mood.*

But it's going to take a lot to make that wish come true.

# A WIND CHANGE

When I walk into the dining room,
everyone from the wedding party is seated
at a special table that's covered with white
flowers, pretty plates, and glasses. It looks
like the kind of table you see when
someone is getting married on TV.

Captain Nate is at one end, and Frank
and Colleen are at the other. Mom, Max,
Mary Ann, Joey, Winnie, Grandpa Winston,
Aunt Alice, and Aunt Emily are on the sides.

Captain Nate pats an empty chair next

to him. "Mallory, we saved this for you."

I sit down between Max and Captain Nate, but when I do, I feel like everyone is giving me a *why-did-you-leave-the-wedding* look instead of a *we-saved-a-chair-for-you* look.

I take a roll out of the basket on the table and look down while I'm buttering it. Even though Dad said not to worry, I am. The last thing I want to do is look up and answer the question that I feel like everyone wants answered.

Captain Nate taps his spoon against his glass. "I'd like to ask a question."

I take a big bite of buttered roll. I don't know what question Captain Nate is going to ask. But if it's *Mallory, why did you leave the wedding of your best friends' parents right as your best friends were becoming a family?* I want to make sure my mouth is too full to answer.

123

But Captain Nate's question surprises me. "Who here thinks that we have the prettiest bride and the most handsome groom on the high seas?"

Everyone laughs and claps when he says that.

Captain Nate walks around the table and stands next to Colleen and Frank, then raises his glass.

"I'd like to propose a toast to Frank and Colleen and their lovely family. Here's to a lifetime of health and happiness and good times," he says.

Dad raises his glass. "I second that," he says.

Grandpa Winston raises his glass. "Can I third it?" he asks.

Everyone laughs and clinks their glasses

together, then Captain Nate sits down.

I swallow my mouthful of buttered roll. I thought for sure Captain Nate was going to ask why I left the wedding. I thought that was what *everyone* was going to want to talk about at this dinner. But that's not what *anybody* is talking about.

In fact, everybody is so busy talking about the wedding ceremony, and how lovely the table looks, and how Frank and Colleen are the perfect bride and groom, and how the Winstons are all a nice, big, family now, that *nobody* seems to want to talk about why I left the wedding at all.

Well . . . almost nobody.

"Hey, Mallory," Max whispers in my ear, "I have a joke for you."

I take a bite of my salad. I don't really want to hear Max's joke, but he tells it anyway.

"Who made like a tree and decided to leaf a wedding?" he says.

I don't ask *who.* Instead I lean across Max. "Mom! Tell Max not to . . . "

I guess Mom heard Max's joke too, because before I can even say *tease me,* Mom tells Max to stop. "This is none of your business," she whispers to Max.

Max starts to open his mouth like he'd like to say something and make it his business, but Mom tells him to eat his salad.

I take a big bite of mine, and look at Mary Ann and Joey.

It's not that I really want to explain why I left, but I would like to know that my best friends care enough to ask why I was gone. But they don't look like they care at all. I watch while Mary Ann gives Joey the olives off of her salad.

Mary Ann and I both hate olives and Joey loves them. I guess now that they're brother and sister, they'll do things like give each other the parts of their salads that they don't like.

I push my olives off to the side of my plate.

"Let's all take a picture," says Colleen.

Everyone stands up and crowds around Colleen and Frank.

I try to smile while Captain Nate takes the picture, but it's hard to smile when your brain is busy thinking about all of the salads your best friends are going to have together now that they're a family.

I sit quietly while a waiter takes away my salad. He puts a plate with chicken and rice and little baby carrots in front of me.

I eat a carrot, and I wait. Before I came to dinner, I didn't want *anyone* to ask me why I left the wedding. Now, I want *someone* to ask. I wait for someone, anyone, to ask why I left.

But no one does.

I watch while Mary Ann and Joey and Winnie give Frank and Colleen the matching hats that they bought for them.

"They're wonderful!" says Colleen to Winnie and Joey and Mary Ann when she opens the box they give her. She puts

the hat on her head, then puts Frank's on his head.

"How do I look?" Frank makes a funny face and grins, and everyone laughs. He and Colleen give Mary Ann and Joey and Winnie big hugs.

I listen while everyone *oohs* and *aahs* about the hats and says what a happy occasion it is when two people get married. I don't think that's always true, because right now, I'm not feeling so happy. I think about what Dad and I talked about on deck. He said that to have a friend you have to be a friend.

I tried. I really did. But Mary Ann and Joey didn't try back.

I watch while Frank passes around the *Winston Crew* T-shirts they made the other day. All of the Winstons slip them on over their wedding clothes, and the photographer takes a picture of them.

I look down at my chicken and rice. Just thinking about all of this makes me feel not hungry.

Captain Nate looks at my plate. "What's the matter Mallory? You don't like the chicken?"

I shake my head. "The chicken is fine," I tell Captain Nate. "I guess I'm just not very hungry."

Captain Nate nods his head like he understands not being hungry. "If you're not going to eat your dinner, why don't I tell you a story instead."

"OK," I tell Captain Nate. But the truth is . . . I'm not really in the mood for chicken or a story. But I listen anyway while Captain Nate starts talking.

"Mallory, when I was just about your age, I got my first boat. My father gave it to me. It was a little sailboat, and I loved it right away."

Captain Nate smiles to himself like adults do sometimes when they're remembering something pleasant from when they were kids.

"During the week, I would come home from school and take care of my boat. On the weekends, my father taught me how to sail it. We would sail together, until eventually I got good enough that he let me take it out on my own. One weekend, when I started out, the skies were blue and there was a nice breeze."

Captain Nate stops smiling. The corners of his mouth turn down, like he's remembering something that wasn't so pleasant.

"Then the wind changed. The skies turned dark and out of nowhere, the wind started blowing in a different direction." Captain Nate stops talking. He looks like he's busy remembering.

"What happened then?" I ask him.

Captain Nate looks at me. "Then my sail started moving from one side of the boat to the other, and before I knew what to do, my boat capsized."

"It fell over?" I ask Captain Nate.

"Yes, it did," he says. "My boat was turned over. I was in the water, and I was kicking and hanging onto the boat and trying to stay afloat."

I didn't know Captain Nate was going to

tell me a scary story. "That must have been awful. What did you do?" I ask.

"I didn't know what to do," says Captain Nate. "I was trying to turn the boat back over and get in it, but I couldn't. Then I saw another boat in the distance. It was my father, in a motorboat. He was coming to rescue me."

"You must have been glad to see him!"

"I was glad and very surprised," says Captain Nate. "I didn't expect the wind to change, and I didn't expect my father to show up and rescue me."

"I see," I say to Captain Nate, even though I'm not quite sure I do see what he means or why he's telling me this story.

I guess Captain Nate can tell I look a little confused, because he keeps talking. "Sometimes," he says, "things seem to be going one way, and then, unexpectedly, they change, and you see that they're really taking a different course."

"Are you talking about the wind?" I ask Captain Nate.

Captain Nate smiles. "The funny thing about the wind is that it's a lot like people. You're never one hundred percent sure what either one of them are going to do."

"I see," I tell Captain Nate. But the truth is, I'm not sure I see at all.

# PARTY TIME

"Party time!" says Frank. He stands up from the table. "Everybody follow me to the *Tuxedo Lounge.* We've got dancing to do!"

Everyone follows Frank to the *Tuxedo Lounge,* and everyone looks like they're in a dancing mood . . . everyone but one person, and that one person is me.

I scrape my party shoes along the deck of the ship as we walk to the party.

When we get to the *Tuxedo Lounge,* Frank

throws open the doors. "Welcome to the party!" he says. When we walk inside, I'm amazed by what I see. There are white flowers everywhere and a real band playing music.

"Everything looks beautiful!" says Colleen.

Frank smiles like he's glad she likes it. He takes her hand and they start dancing. Mom and Dad and Grandpa Winston and Aunt Alice and Aunt Emily and Joey and Mary Ann all join in. Even Winnie and Max start dancing, and I didn't think Max knew how to dance.

I sit down in a chair in a corner and put my purse and camera down next to me. I watch while everyone dances. Looking at all the Winstons in their matching *Winston Crew* T-shirts makes me feel like I'm not part of this party at all.

I look down at my watch. 8:11 P.M.

I think about what Captain Nate said, about how things can change unexpectedly. It doesn't seem like anything is going to change unexpectedly tonight. Not even the minute hand on my watch.

I look down again. 8:13 P.M. This party just started and it feels like I've been here for a week. I wish I had something fun to do.

I cross my right leg over my left. Then I uncross it and put my left over my right. I do it six times, and then I look at my watch again. 8:15 P.M.

I cross and re-cross my legs. I look at my watch while I do it. I try to figure out how many times I can re-cross my legs in an hour. I'm so busy crossing and re-crossing, that I don't even notice when Joey and Mary Ann sit down beside me.

"Hey, Mallory," says Joey. "Mary Ann and I want to know if you'll come out on the deck with us for a minute."

I look at Mary Ann. She's holding something behind her back. "We have a surprise for you," she says.

Before I have a chance to say *Yes, I'll come* or *No, I won't*, Mary Ann and Joey each take one of my arms and walk me out of the *Tuxedo Lounge* onto the upper deck.

139

"Mallory," says Joey, "Mary Ann and I wanted to talk to you because we feel like we owe you an apology."

I don't say anything when Joey says that, because I'm not sure what to say.

But Mary Ann does. "Mallory, everything has been so crazy and exciting ever since Frank and my mom decided to get married. It's like everything changed really fast, and so much happened, and now we're here on this cruise."

I shrug my shoulders. I still don't know what to say.

Joey continues. "You're our best friend, and ever since our parents decided to get married, we've both been so busy being part of that, we feel like we haven't had much time to be a good friend to you."

"The thing is. . . ," I start to tell Joey how left out I felt when they were taking family pictures and making family T-shirts and buying wedding presents for their parents.

But before I can say anything, Mary Ann puts an arm around me. "You're our best, best, best friend, and we're really sorry if we did anything that made you feel left out."

I think about what Captain Nate said about things changing unexpectedly. I definitely wasn't expecting an apology, but getting one makes me feel better. "I feel like I owe you an apology too," I tell Mary Ann and Joey.

They look at each other, and they look confused.

"For what?" Joey asks.

I look down at my party shoes. The toes are all scuffed. "For running out of the wedding when I did. I know that it was a really important time for both of you. It's just that watching my two best friends become a family was kind of hard."

Joey and Mary Ann both smile. "Even though we're part of the same family now, you'll always be our best friend," says Joey.

I smile back at them. "Thanks. And thanks for apologizing. That was a nice surprise."

Mary Ann and Joey look at each other, and they both burst out laughing.

"That wasn't the surprise," says Mary Ann.

She hands me what she's been holding behind her back. "*This* is the surprise."

I look down at the bag Mary Ann is holding. I take it from her and take out the pink tissue paper that's sticking out of the top. Then I take out what's inside. When I do, I start smiling.

"A T-shirt!" I say. I hold it up against my

body and read what's written on it. *BFF of the Winston Crew.* It looks just like the other *Winston Crew* T-shirts.

"That's right," says Mary Ann. "You are the official *Best Friend Forever of the Winston Crew.*"

"We thought you needed a T-shirt," says Joey. "So this morning while Mary Ann and Winnie were getting their hair done, I asked Felix if he would let me back in the art room. I told him there was one more T-shirt we needed to make, and that it was an important one."

I smile at Joey. "So that's what you were doing when you couldn't go swimming?"

Joey nods his head *yes.* "Don't you want to wear your shirt?" he asks.

"I sure do," I say with a big smile. I slip my shirt on over my party dress and put my arms around my best friends.

I think about the wishes I made on deck with Dad. I guess the ocean makes a pretty good wish pond, because I feel like they're both coming true.

"Who's ready to party?" I ask.

Mary Ann and Joey nod their heads like they both are, and we all walk back into the *Tuxedo Lounge.*

When we come back in, everybody crowds around us.

"Great shirt!" says Frank.

"Do you want me to take a picture of the three of you together with your camera?" Dad asks me.

"Sure," I say.

Dad snaps a few pictures of us together, and then he gives me the camera.

I didn't think I would want to take pictures tonight, but I take lots of pictures at the party of everyone dancing and laughing and eating wedding cake.

When the party is almost over, Felix and Captain Nate come into the room.

"Congratulations!" Felix says to Frank and Colleen.

When he sees me wearing my T-shirt, he grins. "How do you like your surprise?"

"I love it!" I tell Felix. And I do love it. From the moment I put it on, I haven't been able to stop smiling.

Captain Nate smiles at me. "Looks like there's been a wind change and the night is ending on a

good note," he says.

But when he says that, I stop smiling. "It's time for the night to end?" I can't believe the fun has to stop.

Captain Nate pats me on the head. "I'm afraid the party is over," he says.

Then Mary Ann puts her arm around me. "But another one is just beginning."

# PJ'S & POPCORN

"I didn't think we'd get to have a pajama party on the cruise ship."

Mary Ann throws a piece of popcorn in the air and catches it in her mouth. "I'm glad we brought our matching palm tree PJ's."

I'm glad too, because these PJ's couldn't be any more perfect for our first and only pajama party in Mary Ann's state room on board the *Sea Queen*. "It's so cool that your mom said I could sleep over tonight."

Mary Ann giggles. "I don't know how much sleeping we'll get done. This cot is pretty little for both of us."

I throw a piece of popcorn in the air. I try to catch it in my mouth, but it lands in my hair instead. Mary Ann and I both laugh while I try to pick it out.

"So what do you want to do?" asks Mary Ann. "We can watch a movie or make hot chocolate in the microwave."

I love movies and hot chocolate, but tonight, there's something else I want to do. Even though I feel much better since Joey and Mary Ann apologized and gave me the T-shirt, Mary Ann is my lifelong best friend, and there's still something I want to talk to her about.

"Maybe we can just talk," I say to Mary Ann. But when I try to start, I feel like someone glued my mouth shut. Even though I've known Mary Ann since the day I was born, and we've always been able to talk about everything, I'm having a hard time getting this conversation started.

"I think I know what you want to talk about," says Mary Ann.

"You do?" I don't know why I'm surprised that Mary Ann would. She knows me better than anyone.

"You want to talk about how much fun it's going to be when the school year is over and Mom and I move to Fern Falls and we're neighbors again."

I fill my mouth with popcorn and chew it slowly. "That's sort of it," I say to Mary Ann when I'm done chewing.

I fluff up my pillow and sit on it so I'm more comfy. "The thing is . . . I am excited about you moving to Fern Falls. But I'm kind of scared too."

Mary Ann makes a face, an *I'm-not-sure-I-understand-what-you're-talking-about* face, so I explain.

"Ever since we came on the cruise, you and Joey and Winnie have been doing stuff together." I remind Mary Ann about the T-shirts and the wedding presents and the matching hairstyles and all the other things they've done, like sitting together at dinner and being in the *Welcome Aboard* show, that I haven't gotten to do.

I look down at the pillow I'm sitting on. It doesn't feel very fluffy. "Seeing you do all those things with them made me feel left out. And I'm scared that when you move to Fern Falls, you'll always be doing things with them because they'll be your family, and I'll always be left out."

When I finish, I wait. I wait for Mary Ann to say, *Awww, Mallory don't worry. You'll always be my best, best, best friend and I'll never leave you out of anything.*

But that's not what Mary Ann says. She doesn't say a word.

I wait for her to say something, but Mary Ann is silent. She looks down at a piece of popcorn she's holding and squishes it between her fingers.

When she looks up, I see something I don't see often . . . Mary Ann is crying.

I watch as the tears roll down her cheeks. "What's the matter?" I ask softly.

"You're not the only one who's scared," Mary Ann says. Her voice is barely a whisper. "Do you remember how you felt when you had to move to Fern Falls?"

I nod my head *yes*. I do remember. "I was
scared," I tell Mary Ann. "There were so
many new things in my life. A new house. A
new neighborhood. A new school."

Mary Ann wipes her eyes on the sleeve of
her pajamas. "I have all of that plus a new
brother and a new sister and a new father
and a new grandfather. And when I move
to Fern Falls, I'll have to share my mom
with two other kids."

When Mary Ann says that, she really starts crying.

I hadn't thought about how all of this would make Mary Ann feel, but I can understand why she's feeling so upset and scared.

I reach across the cot and give Mary Ann the world's biggest hug. But when I do, she starts crying even harder.

"If you keep crying," I say softly, "the palm trees on your PJ's are going to think they got caught in rainstorm."

When I say that, Mary Ann stops crying and starts laughing. Once she starts, she can't stop. When she finally does, she looks at me seriously. "Do you know what I think the best part of moving to Fern Falls will be?"

I shake my head *no*. I'm not sure what she thinks will be the best part.

"Living next door to you again and being best friends," she says.

When she says that, it makes me feel like I'm going to cry. "Things will be just like they used to be," I say. "We can chew the same kind of gum and paint our nails the same color and say everything three times."

Mary Ann grins. "Let's pinky swear," she says.

We lift up our right pinkies and hook them around each other.

"Best friends," says Mary Ann.

"Forever," I say.

When we finish our pinky swear, Mary Ann reaches over and turns off the little light beside her cot. "Good night, sleep tight, and don't let the bedbugs bite," she says.

I smile when she says it. That's what we

always say to each other right before we go to sleep. But tonight, it feels weird.

I sit up in bed. "Hey, Mary Ann, I have a question," I whisper in the dark.

"What is it?" she asks.

"Do you think there are bedbugs on ships?"

Mary Ann giggles. "I don't know," she says. "But if there are, I guess they'd have to swim to get on board."

I giggle back. Somehow I don't think Captain Nate and Felix would let them on board the *Sea Queen*.

# LAND, HO!

I put scrambled eggs, bacon, hash browns, and four pancakes on my plate.

Max looks down at my plate and gives me an *I've-never-seen-anyone-eat-so-much-for-breakfast* look. "Leave some for the rest of the people on board," he says.

"There's plenty for everyone," Grandpa Winston says to Max.

I give Max a *Grandpa-Winston-knows-more-than-you-do-so-keep-your-rude-comments-to-yourself* look. "Since today is our last day, I don't want to miss out on a thing," I tell Max. I help myself to some strawberries.

Joey is in line behind me. He takes a bagel and spreads butter and jelly on it. "I'm *so* sad that today is our last day on the ship."

Mary Ann puts a waffle on her plate and squirts it with whipped cream. "I'm *so, so* sad," she says.

I pour syrup all over my pancakes. "I'm *so, so, so* sad," I say. I'm also so, so, so sleepy. Mary Ann and I had a lot of fun last night, but we didn't get a lot of sleep.

I yawn as we carry our plates to the table. Even though I'm sad, sad, sad that the cruise is almost over, I'm happy too. It didn't start out great for me, but it ended up being so much fun.

"We have a lot of people to say good-bye to," Joey says as we sit down.

"And one of those people is right here," booms a deep voice behind us.

I turn around. "Captain Nate!"

He smiles at all of us. "It's been fun having the three of you on board."

"Thanks for *everything,* Captain Nate." I say *everything* like Captain Nate knows exactly what that means, and I think he does.

"You are quite welcome, Mallory." Captain Nate tips his hat in my direction and winks at me. "Stay alert. You never know when the wind might change. Good luck to all of you," he says before he moves on to say good-bye to the people at the next table.

Mary Ann and Joey and I start on our breakfast.

"I can't believe that the next meal we have will be on land," Mary Ann says

between bites of waffle.

"I'll tell you what I can't believe," says Joey. "I can't believe we have to leave behind the breakfast buffet." He stuffs part of a bagel into his mouth. "Maybe when you and your mom move to Fern Falls, she'll make a breakfast buffet one day," Joey says to Mary Ann.

Mary Ann laughs. "The only thing my mom knows how to make are frozen waffles."

"I guess we can have a frozen waffle buffet," says Joey.

Mary Ann laughs when he says that.

Even though I don't love the idea of Joey and Mary Ann eating frozen waffles together, I try not to think about them doing that. Instead, I think about how much fun it will be when Mary Ann moves to Fern Falls and lives next door to me.

"Hey, let's go find Felix," I say. I stand up from the table and motion for Joey and Mary Ann to follow me. "He must be up on the deck."

We walk outside. But before we have a chance to find Felix, someone finds us.

"Hey, guys!" Tammy waves to us. "I can't believe today is our last day on the ship! I saw a TV show one time about this ship, and right before the ship gets to land, it hits a big rock and . . ."

But before Tammy can tell us what happens to the ship, Felix comes up behind us. "Who wants a balloon?" he asks.

Before any of us can say *Yes we do* or *No we don't,* Felix gives us all helium balloons with the *Sea Queen* logo on them.

Joey gets a red one. Mary Ann gets a yellow one. Tammy gets a green one. And I get a big purple balloon.

"Thanks," we all say to Felix.

"I hope you all had a wonderful time aboard the *Sea Queen*," he says.

"We had a great time," says Mary Ann.

Felix gives me a *does-that-include-you* look, and I nod my head. "We *all* had a good time," I tell him.

Felix rumples my hair. "I'm so glad to hear it. We don't want any of our guests to go home unhappy," he says.

"The only thing we're unhappy about is that we have to go home," I tell Felix.

He laughs. "How about one last picture before you go?"

He walks us over to where Candace, the official photographer of the *Sea Queen,* is taking pictures. She lines us up with our balloons in front of the fake palm trees.

"Big smile!" says Candace. "When I count to three, I want you all to say . . ."

But before she can say *cheeseburger,* we all do . . . even me.

Felix claps his hands like he's applauding our picture-taking abilities. "That was a great shot," he says. "Now, I have one last thing to show you." Felix points to the outline of buildings on the horizon.

I look in the direction he's pointing. The buildings on the shore look like they're getting closer by the minute.

"We'll be there before you know it," says Felix.

Mary Ann puts her arm through mine. We walk over to the edge of the deck and watch as the buildings get bigger and bigger.

"Land, ho!" says Mary Ann. She laughs at her joke.

But I don't. There's only one thing I have to say to that: *Land, no!*

I wish there was some way that I could slow the ship down. I look out at the ocean and make one more wish. *I wish the cruise didn't have to end.*

Even though the ocean makes a great wish pond, I know there's no hope of my last wish coming true.

"Hey," says Mary Ann.  "Should we let our balloons go?"

I count to three, and at the same time, we let go.  Then we watch as our balloons float happily out of sight.

"What do you think will happen to them?" Mary Ann asks me.

I shrug my shoulders.  "I don't know," I say.

And for that matter, I guess nobody knows what might happen in the future. But standing on the deck of this boat looking out at the sparkly ocean, I just have a feeling that whatever happens, it's going to be good.

# AN ASSIGNMENT

Mrs. Daily's
Assignment of the Day

Please write about what you did over Spring Break. Be specific. Give details. Feel free to include illustrations. End your report by telling us if you liked what you did and why. I can't wait to hear about your experience.

# A Trip Report

## By Reporting Officer Mallory McDonald

Most reports are hard to write, but not this one.

I just got back from a cruise on the Sea Queen. In case you don't know what that is, I will tell you. It's a great big ship and it looks like this:

I did lots of exciting stuff when I was
on the ship, and I'll
tell you about
that too.

I went to a
tropical island.
I attended a
fancy wedding.
And I ate dinner
with the captain of the ship.

I liked what I did very much. At first, I wasn't too thrilled because it seemed like nothing was going my way. Then, Captain Nate told me a story about how things, like the wind and people, can change unexpectedly. And guess what? He was right. Then I lived happily ever after (until the end of the cruise).

## The End

P.S. I don't know if you can put a P.S. on a school report, but I am anyway. Even though I loved the cruise and I was sorry it had to end, coming home wasn't so bad because my cat, Cheeseburger, was so, so, so happy to see me.

*Mallory, I'm so glad you enjoyed your trip and your homecoming! Grade: A+ P.S. I've never had a student add a P.S. to a school report, but I'm glad you did. I liked it so, so, so much! —Mrs. Daily*

# A SPECIAL SCRAPBOOK

You'll never believe what I'm making! A special scrapbook for Mary Ann and Joey and Winnie with pictures I took from the party.

I'm putting in a picture of Colleen and Frank dancing.

I'm putting in a picture of Mary Ann and Winnie and Joey dancing.

And I'm putting in a picture of everyone eating wedding cake.

I also have a picture that Dad took with my camera of me with Mary Ann and Joey.

I know what you're thinking: That even though I had a hard time with the whole *Colleen-and-Frank-getting-married-and-Joey-*

and-Mary-Ann-becoming-part-of-the-same-crew
thing, I look like I'm having a pretty good
time in the picture.

The truth is . . . the party was a lot of
fun. Even though I'm not part of the
Winston Crew, I'm the BFF of the Winston
Crew. With friends like Mary Ann and Joey,
I can't think of a better thing to be!

Carolrhoda Books, Inc.
A division of Lerner Publishing Group
241 First Avenue North
Minneapolis, MN 55401 U.S.A.

Website address: www.lernerbooks.com


Library of Congress Cataloging-in-Publication Data

Friedman, Laurie B.
      Mallory on board / by Laurie Friedman ; illustrations by Barbara Pollak.
         p. cm.
      Summary: Despite her fears of being a "third wheel," Mallory goes on a
  cruise for the wedding of the mother and father of her two best friends.
      ISBN-13: 978-0-8225-6194-1 (lib. bdg. : alk. paper)
      ISBN-10: 0-8225-6194-8 (lib. bdg. : alk. paper)
      [1. Remarriage—Fiction. 2. Cruise ships—Fiction. 3. Best friends—Fiction.
  4. Friendship—Fiction. 5. Family life—Fiction.]  I. Pollak, Barbara, ill. II. Title.
  PZ7.F89773Mai 2007
  [Fic]—dc22                                                      2006013841

Manufactured in the United States of America
1 2 3 4 5 6 — BP — 12 11 10 09 08 07